P9-BBV-197

Olive's Pirate Party

by ROBERTA BAKER

Illustrated by DEBBIE TILLEY

For Hug Bug and Swamp Thing,
with love always. 1 Cor. 13

—R.B.

For Emma Rose Rowell
—D.T.

Little, Brown and Company
Time Warner Book Group
1271 Avenue of the Americas, New York, NY 10020
Visit our Web site at www.lb-kids.com

First Edition

Library of Congress Cataloging-in-Publication Data

Baker, Roberta.
Olive's pirate party / by Roberta Baker ; illustrated by Debbie Tilley. — 1st ed.
p. cm.
Summary: Olive worries that having her seventh-birthday pirate party at her Aunt Tiffany's house will be a disappointment.
ISBN 0-316-16792-4
[1. Aunts—Fiction. 2. Pirates—Fiction. 3. Birthdays—Fiction. 4. Parties—Fiction.] I. Tilley, Debbie, ill. II. Title.
PZ7.B17485Ol 2005
[E]—dc22 2004004703

10 9 8 7 6 5 4 3 2 1

SC

Manufactured in China

The illustrations for this book were done in watercolor and ink.
The text was set in Fairfield and Providence, and the title was handlettered by Holly Dickens.

When Olive Elizabeth Julia Jerome turned seven, she wanted a party with pirates.

"Mom and Dad, instead of candles, can I have cannons on my birthday cake?"

At school, she stood on the climbing tower and passed out invitations.

Ahoy, mateys! It's Captain Olive! I'm having a pirate party with swordfights, a gangplank, buried treasure, a lagoon filled with alligators...

"Cool!" said Olive's friend Lizard. "Can I bring my snorkeling mask?"

Meanwhile, Olive's parents were frantic.

"Only five days left until Olive's birthday! Where can we bury the treasure? The house painters will be here. . . . The yard is dug up. . . ."

"Why not have Olive's party at my house?" trilled Olive's Aunt Tiffany. "Leave everything to me."

Aunt Tiffany was Olive's elderly aunt. She sewed satin gowns for Olive's dolls, baked petit fours for her stuffed animals' birthdays, and took Olive to the opera when she turned six—and translated everything.

"If I know Aunt Tiffany, your party will be something special," chimed Olive's mom.

But the thought gave Olive goose bumps. Aunt Tiffany's house was like a museum.

"What if the pirates break something? To Aunt Tiffany, *special* means teacups and lace and scary food on fancy plates—not swordfights!" Olive slumped. "Sounds like my plans have walked the plank."

"I can't wait for your party," Lizard chirped the next day at school. "I'll wear my octopus bathing suit. Dad says I can borrow his metal detector to find the buried treasure!"

Olive gulped. "There's been a change in plans."

"The party's at your old Aunt Tiffany's?" hissed Hillary, goalie for the soccer team. "That means no buccaneer burgers? And no gangplank jump??"

"Sounds like your birthday could be a disaster." Olive's friend Errol shook his head. "Want to spend the day in my underground fort? We could eat mud pies instead of cake."

"I wish I never said anything about a dumb old pirate party," Olive groaned.

"Sweetheart, Aunt Tiffany loves you," piped her mom. "I'm sure everyone will have lots of fun."

"I wish I had an Aunt Tiffany who loved me enough to give me a party," echoed Olive's dad.

ANY TWOS?
Go fish dear..
Heart and Sou
TRICK OR TREAT
HAVE YOU FL

That night, Olive couldn't sleep. She hugged Gumbo, her polar bear, closed her eyes, and kept thinking about Aunt Tiffany.

"I love Aunt Tiffany, and she loves me," announced Olive.

So if I'm going to have a party with pirates, I'll just bring them to Aunt Tiffany's house . . . and we'll redecorate!

The next day, when Ms. Fishbone's class made papier-mâché masks, Olive made Blackbeard the Pirate.

In science, when they painted an ocean mural, Olive was in charge of the details.

"Ms. Fishbone, can I please borrow this mural on Saturday if I do extra-credit spelling homework?"

At lunch, Olive stood on a cafeteria bench and made an important announcement.

All hands on deck! Prepare to cast off on Saturday! Dress like pirates and dig for treasure! And don't forget your toy sharks!!

"The pirate party's back on?" Lizard sparkled.

"Are you *sure* it's going to be fun?" Hillary snorted.

"Anything else, Miss Jerome?" Mr. Weepole, the principal, rocked on his heels.

Olive blushed. "Mr. Weepole, do you know where I can find a giant white teacup?"

The night before Olive's party, Aunt Tiffany vacuumed and rearranged. She packed her crystal goblets and china plates.

Breakable"
Figurines"

The next morning, Olive woke up at sunrise.
She watched the second hand sweep the clock.

Cock-a-doodle doo, Mom and Dad! I just turned seven! Time to put candles in the donuts! Last one to the table gets a runny fried egg!

After breakfast, Olive worked in her tree house.

Then she sailed to Aunt Tiffany's doorstep.

"I hope we don't have to eat broccoli," Hillary grumbled.

"Is it okay to swing from the yardarm?" Lizard squeaked.

“What real treasure??” a gravelly voice thundered.

Aunt Tiffany’s door creaked open.

Aunt Tiffany stood, transformed, hands on hips, flashing a blackened tooth.

“I-is that you, Aunt Tiffany?” Olive sputtered.

"Aunt Tiffany," Olive bubbled, "you look just like Bluebeard the Pirate! Now all you need is a ship!"

"I do?" Aunt Tiffany stared.

"Full speed ahead!" Olive spouted.

Together they turned the living room into a pirate galleon.

I was wondering what to do with Uncle Albert...

In Aunt Tiffany's tub, they trolled for gold coins.

In her closets, they combed for treasure.

Then everyone sat down to Jolly Roger cake that Aunt Tiffany had baked.

"Look, Olive's cake even has cannons!"

"Aunt Tiffany, this is the best party ever!" Olive thought for a minute. "But where did you put all your teacups?"

Aunt Tiffany smiled slyly and winked. "Pirates don't use *teacups*, dear!"

After Olive opened her presents, Aunt Tiffany opened one from Olive.

"Olive Elizabeth Julia Jerome!"

"I painted it myself," said Olive.

"You're no ordinary pirate!" Aunt Tiffany squeezed Olive's hand.

"You're no ordinary Aunt Tiffany. . . ." Olive squeezed Aunt Tiffany back.

"...Aunt Tiffany? Instead of nine pirates, can I invite twenty-nine next year?"
I told you Olive's party would have an anti-gravity machine.
Look, I found it! Buried treasure!